Your Guide to
Superheroes

Lee Aucoin, *Creative Director*
Jamey Acosta, *Senior Editor*
Heidi Fiedler, *Editor*
Produced and designed by
Denise Ryan & Associates
Illustration © Tom Bonson
Rachelle Cracchiolo, *Publisher*

Teacher Created Materials

5301 Oceanus Drive
Huntington Beach, CA 92649-1030
http://www.tcmpub.com
Paperback: ISBN: 978-1-4333-5566-0
Library Binding: ISBN: 978-1-4807-1711-4
© 2014 Teacher Created Materials

D0166557

Written by James Reid
Illustrated by Tom Bonson

ACHOO!

Contents

Are you tired of carrying heavy books?
Do you need help with homework?
Or pesky younger brothers?
Hire a superhero!

From head to toe, our team is the best!
There's no problem these heroes can't fix.
So take a look at all their tricks and make your pick.
Call 888-555-HERO to book yours today!

5

Super Shoulders

Never be weighed down by your backpack again. Strong shoulders means Dr. Bear can carry just about anything. Trains? Planes? Cars? You name it! She will even carry pets that are too tired to walk.

Claim to Fame

Dr. Bear once carried a pet rhino home from school. The rhino was exhausted after Show and Tell. Of course, everyone has their limits. Dr. Bear would rather forget dropping the rhino in the pool!

Dr. Bear

Large Lungs

Mr. Puff is famous for his huge lungs. He can swim underwater for hours! He is an expert at fetching things from the bottom of the pool. He even saved the rhino! He likes to relax by playing the trombone for hours.

Claim to Fame

Mr. Puff is best known for playing nine trombones at the same time! *Parp! Parp!*

So Smart

Sir Smart's brain works so quickly he can answer any question in a flash. Ask him anything! He is very good at "knock knock" jokes, too.

Claim to Fame

This is his most famous joke:

Knock knock.

Who's there?

Cash.

Cash who?

No, but I would like a peanut instead!

Sir Smart

Soft and Stretchy

Can't reach that button? Call Duke Digit. His fingers and toes are awfully flexible. His fingers can fetch things way under the fridge. And he can twiddle his toes so quickly he can beat eggs into omelets.

Claim to Fame

The Duke once knitted four sweaters at the same time! He only wore one at a time though.

Duke Digit

13

Not a Normal Nose

Sam Snell's nose is powerful. He can make any bad smell into a good smell. He's an expert with dirty gym shoes. Give him your barf. Make him sort through your trash. He makes anything smell like daisies. You won't be disappointed.

Claim to Fame

Sam Snell is famous for making a school smell fresh again after a science experiment went very, very wrong.

Sam Snell

15

Super Sonic

Pssst! Whether you're quietly watching TV on the sly or trying to hear a friend whisper, Audi Tory can help. Her ears are so strong she can hear an ant sneeze. With her help, you'll never miss a word again.

Claim to Fame

Audi once heard a toenail grow. She caught it early and warned her client before the toenail made a hole in her sock.

Audi Tory

17

Exceptional Eyeballs

Is your room a mess? Do you need a magnifying glass to find your homework? Call Super Ray and use his super sight. He is an expert at finding lost cats, books, shoes, and odd socks. Audi Tory and Super Ray often work as a team. Book them now and get two heroes for the price of one!

Claim to Fame

Super Ray's most famous feat was finding a hundred pairs of odd socks. They had been in the back of a closet for over two years. Wow!

Super Ray

19

Dial a Dream

Have trouble sleeping? Call a superhero to chase the monsters away. Ms. Vera Alert is an expert at making hot chocolate and tucking children into bed. Her bedtime stories are long and dreamy. She never sleeps at night. But you will!

Claim to Fame

Ms. Alert once lulled a group of excited children to sleep at camp. A good night's rest did them good. And the next day, they climbed a mountain faster than ever!

Ms. Vera Alert

21

Happy Helper

Feeling down? Topsy Turvy turns bad times into good times. She is an expert at fixing toys ruined by little brothers. And she can make the sun come out on rainy days.

Claim to Fame

When the local basketball team lost every game last year, they called Topsy. With her help, they won the first game of the season. This year, they may be champions. Topsy really turned things around!

Topsy Turvy

23

Lots of Love

Dr. Hart Beat has a huge heart. He loves everything! Plants, animals, messy boys, and silly girls—he loves them all! And that makes everyone happy.

Claim to Fame

Want to join the team? Dr. Beat is famous for teaching normal people how to be superheroes.

Dr. Hart Beat

So, why not call a superhero?
It's so easy to do.

Our next superhero could be YOU!